Pony-Sitters

Do you love ponies? Be a Pony Pal!

Pony Pals

Pony-Sitters

Jeanne Betancourt

illustrated by Paul Bachem

A
LITTLE APPLE
PAPERBACK

SCHOLASTIC INC.
New York Toronto London Auckland Sydney

ISBN 0-590-86601-X

Text copyright © 1997 by Jeanne Betancourt.
Illustrations copyright © 1997 by Paul Bachem.
All rights reserved. Published by Scholastic Inc.
LITTLE APPLE PAPERBACKS and PONY PALS are trademarks and/or registered trademarks of Scholastic Inc.

24 23 22 21 20 19 18   7 8 9/0

Printed in the U.S.A.   40

First Scholastic printing, March 1997

Thank you to Anika Murray — artist and Pony Pal.

Also, thank you to Alyson, Lindsay, and Allyssa Latour for sharing their love and knowledge of ponies. Allyssa has a small Shetland pony named Puffin.

Contents

Pony-Sitters

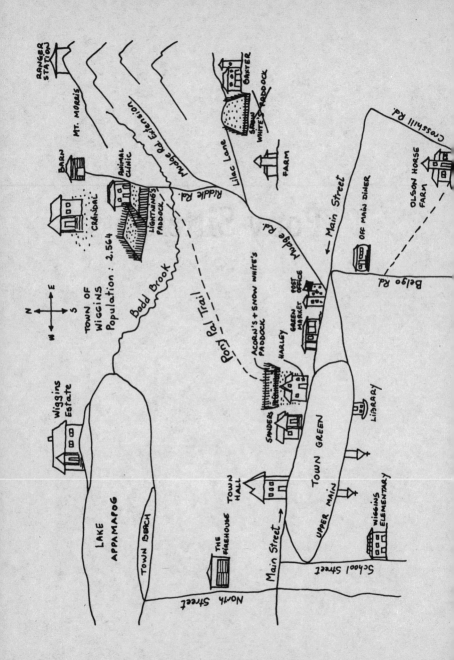

The Smallest Pony

It was a beautiful Thursday afternoon and Anna Harley was studying with her tutor. Anna couldn't wait for the lesson to end. She wanted to be riding her pony, Acorn.

When the lesson was finally over, Anna raced home. She changed into her riding clothes and went out to the backyard. "Acorn," she called to her Shetland pony. Acorn ran across the paddock and Anna gave him a big hug. "We're going for a trail ride," she said happily.

"Hi, Anna," a voice called out. Anna looked up. Her neighbors, Mr. and Mrs. Kline, were walking toward her. Anna went up to the fence to meet them. Acorn walked along behind her.

Mrs. Kline reached over the fence and patted Acorn on the neck.

Acorn nickered as if to say, "That feels good."

"What a sweet pony," said Mrs. Kline.

"Mimi loves Acorn, too," said Anna.

"She loved that pony ride you gave her," Mrs. Kline said.

"I remember the pony rides you and your friends had at the Firehouse Fair," said Mr. Kline. "You were all very responsible."

"Mimi talks about ponies all the time," said Mrs. Kline. "She's even started drawing pictures of them."

Anna smoothed the mane on Acorn's forehead. "I like to draw ponies, too."

"We're thinking of giving Mimi a pony

for her birthday," Mr. Kline said. "She turns five tomorrow."

"Mr. Olson has a darling little Shetland for sale," added Mrs. Kline.

"I got Acorn from Olson's Horse Farm," Anna told them. "I know lots of people who've bought ponies and horses from Mr. Olson."

"Well, the pony we saw is even smaller than Acorn," Mrs. Kline said. "He's the smallest pony I've ever seen, Anna. And he is so *cute*."

"We'd like to buy the pony for Mimi," said Mr. Kline. "But we need someone to take care of the pony when Mimi's with him. We're busy at the hardware store. And our babysitter, Mrs. Bell, doesn't know the first thing about horses.

"So we wondered if you and your friends could watch Mimi and the pony, say for an hour a day," Mr. Kline continued. "Of course we'd pay you."

"Mrs. Bell would be at the house when

you're there," explained Mrs. Kline. "Your job would be to teach Mimi how to take care of a pony and show her some of the basics of riding."

"If you girls agree to pony-sit," said Mr. Kline, "we'll buy the pony for Mimi."

"We can do it," said Anna. Acorn nuzzled Anna's shoulder. "Acorn can help, too."

Mrs. Kline shook hands with Anna. "It's a deal then. We'll buy the pony and you and your friends will work with Mimi and her new pony an hour a day."

"We call ourselves the Pony Pals," said Anna.

"Well, maybe you can turn our Mimi into a Pony Pal, too," said Mrs. Kline with a grin.

"We'll tell Mr. Olson to deliver the pony at four o'clock tomorrow," said Mr. Kline. "Mimi is going to be one happy little girl."

They turned to go. Mrs. Kline looked over her shoulder and smiled at Anna. "By the way," she said, "the pony's name is Tongo."

"*Tongo!*" exclaimed Anna. "That is such a cute name!"

"A cute name for a cute pony," said Mrs. Kline.

After the Klines left, Anna saddled up Acorn. She checked her watch. She had to hurry. Pam Crandal and Lulu Sanders and their ponies, Lightning and Snow White, were meeting her on Pony Pal Trail.

Anna pulled down the stirrups and mounted. "I can't wait to tell Lulu and Pam about our first pony-sitting job," she told Acorn. "I hope they think it's a good idea, too."

Anna rode onto Pony Pal Trail through the gate at the end of the paddock. The mile-and-a-half trail cut through the woods that separated Acorn and Snow White's paddock from Lightning's paddock. The Pony Pals used the trail to go back and forth to one another's houses.

"Pam and Lulu are meeting us at the

three birch trees," Anna told Acorn. "And we're late." She directed Acorn to move into a canter.

Just then, Anna saw Pam and Lulu cantering toward her. Anna slowed Acorn to a walk. Lulu and Pam slowed their ponies down, too. The three girls met on the trail.

"Is everything all right?" Pam asked Anna.

"We were worried when you were late," said Lulu.

"Everything's great!" said Anna. "I have a surprise for you."

"What?" asked Pam and Lulu in unison.

Anna told Lulu and Pam all about Mimi, Tongo, and the pony-sitting job.

"That sounds like so much fun," said Lulu.

"I can't wait!" exclaimed Pam.

"I knew you'd want to do it," said Anna.

"Let's ride over to the brook and talk about our new job," said Lulu.

The girls rode up to the three birches and turned onto the trail that led into the

Wiggins Estate. Ms. Wiggins was a good friend of the Pony Pals. She let them ride on her land anytime. The Wiggins trails were the perfect place for Pony Pal adventures.

The girls rode over to their favorite spot at Badd Brook. While the ponies drank from the brook, the Pony Pals sat on a big rock to talk.

"I've been thinking," said Pam. "Watching a little kid and a pony is a big responsibility."

"We'll have to be very organized," said Lulu. "And plan out what to teach Mimi during each lesson."

"I hope he's a well behaved pony," said Pam. "Small ponies can be spoiled."

"I rode a small pony when I was Mimi's age," said Lulu. "He was impossible to control. His name was Bubble. All the kids at the stable called him *Trouble*."

"I want to meet Tongo," said Pam. "We should ask Mr. Olson all about him."

"Let's ride over to his horse farm right

after school tomorrow," suggested Lulu.

"Good idea," said Anna.

The Pony Pals led their ponies away from the brook. "We'd better go back," Pam said. "It's almost dinnertime."

Anna wondered what Tongo would be like. What if they couldn't control the small pony? What if Tongo was trouble?

Happy Birthday, Mimi!

After school the next day, the Pony Pals rode over to Belgo Road. They turned onto the woodland trail that was a shortcut to Mr. Olson's farm.

Anna spotted Mr. Olson in front of the barn. He was grooming the smallest pony she'd ever seen.

The girls dismounted and led their ponies toward Mr. Olson.

"That Shetland is adorable," said Lulu. "I love his blond mane and tail."

"Look how still he's standing to be

groomed," added Pam. "He's not even cross-tied."

"So it's the Pony-sitting Pals," Mr. Olson said with a smile.

Acorn pulled on the reins. He wanted to get closer to Tongo. "Will Tongo be okay if Acorn goes up to him?" asked Anna.

"Sure," said Mr. Olson. "Tongo is the sweetest pony to come through this farm."

"Sweeter than Acorn?" asked Anna.

"Your Mr. Acorn can be *very* stubborn," said Mr. Olson.

Anna remembered how stubborn Acorn was when she first had him. "He's not so stubborn anymore," Anna told Mr. Olson. "We're a team now."

Acorn whinnied as if to say, "You know it."

Everyone laughed.

Acorn moved closer to Tongo. The small pony looked up at Acorn and nickered. The two Shetland ponies sniffed one another's faces.

"They're friends already," said Lulu.

"Acorn's going to help us pony-sit," Anna told Mr. Olson.

"I was going to trailer Tongo over to the Klines'," said Mr. Olson. "But if you girls are going back that way, you could pony him beside Acorn. I think this little fellow would like that."

"It would be a great way to surprise Mimi," said Lulu.

"You girls can ride back on the trail," said Mr. Olson. "I'll bring Tongo's tack and other supplies in my pickup truck."

Pam and Lightning took the lead on the trail that led to Belgo Road. Anna followed on Acorn with Tongo ponied behind them. Lulu and Snow White went last.

Anna noticed that Tongo stayed just the right distance behind Acorn and stopped whenever Acorn stopped. Tongo is a perfect pony, thought Anna. Mimi is going to be so excited when she finds out he's *her* pony.

Anna remembered the first time she saw Acorn. Acorn's eyes sparkled, and he was full of energy. When she stroked his neck he nickered at her as if to say, "Choose me!" Mr. Olson showed Anna and her parents three other ponies. But Anna knew that Acorn was the perfect pony for her.

Anna also remembered how her parents gave Acorn back to Mr. Olson because she wasn't making good grades in school. That's when Anna learned that she was having trouble with reading and math because she was dyslexic. The problem wasn't because she was spending too much time with her pony. Anna just needed some extra help. Now she had a tutor *and* her pony.

When it came to school, Pam and Anna were opposites. Pam Crandal loved school and got all A's on her report cards. Anna and Pam were the same, though, about loving ponies and horses. They both loved horses since they were little. Pam's mother was a riding teacher and her father was a veterinarian. They gave Pam her own pony when she was even younger than Mimi Kline. Anna got her pony when she was nine years old.

Lulu Sanders was the last of the three Pony Pals to have her own pony. Lulu's father was a naturalist who traveled all over the world studying wild animals. Lulu's mother died when she was little, so Lulu used to travel with her father. But when Lulu turned ten, her father decided she should live in one place. That's when Lulu came to Wiggins to live with her grandmother. Now that Lulu lived in one place, her dad said she could have a pony. Grandmother Sanders' house was right next to Anna's house, so it was easy for Acorn and Snow White to be stablemates.

The parade of ponies turned off Main Street and climbed the little hill to Upper Main Street where the Klines lived. Anna saw Mimi playing kickball with her mother on the front lawn. Mr. Kline was chatting with Mr. Olson by the pickup truck.

When Mimi saw the Pony Pals riding toward her, she ran to the sidewalk and waved. The Pony Pals halted their ponies in front of her. Anna, Pam, and Lulu sang "Happy Birthday." Mimi stared at Tongo the whole time they were singing. Mrs. Kline knelt down beside her daughter and pointed to the small pony. "That pony is your birthday present," she said with a huge smile.

"My pony!" shouted Mimi. She ran toward Tongo. Mrs. Kline ran behind her. Before she could stop Mimi, the little girl threw her arms around Tongo's neck. "My pony," she cooed to the tiny Shetland. "Mine. Mine. Mine."

Anna was afraid that Tongo would step on Mimi. But the little pony stood still and allowed Mimi to hug him.

A few minutes later, Lulu and Pam led their ponies and Acorn over to the Harley paddock. Mr. and Mrs. Kline were helping Mr. Olson carry the tack and other supplies to the backyard.

Anna and Mimi led Tongo up the driveway toward the backyard. Mimi tugged on Anna's shirt. "I want to ride my pony," she said. "I want to ride him now."

"Not yet," said Anna. "We have to put away his things and check out the tack."

"He's *my* pony," said Mimi.

"I know he's yours," Anna told Mimi. "But we have to take one step at a time."

"He took a lot of steps already," Mimi said.

Anna laughed. "I meant we have to take one *lesson* at a time," she explained.

Mimi put her head against her pony's side. When he felt the little girl's body, he halted. Tongo was already taking good care of his new owner.

"Do you know your pony's name?" Anna asked.

"What's his name?" Mimi asked back.

"Tongo," said Anna. "Isn't that a cute name?"

"I know his name," said Mimi. "He's Tongo. He's *my* pony."

Anna led Tongo in a big circle around the edge of his new backyard home. Anna thought Mimi was walking right behind her. But she wasn't. She was behind Tongo. "Giddyap, Tongo!" Mimi yelled. Mimi was shaking Tongo's tail like cart-driving reins.

"Drop his tail," Anna said in a stern voice. Just then, Anna saw Lulu and Pam running toward them.

Pam reached Mimi first. "Tongo doesn't like it when you stand behind him," she told her. Pam placed her hands over Mimi's, but Mimi still held on to the tail. "Let go!" Pam said.

Mimi finally dropped the tail. But she glared at the Pony Pals. "He's *my* pony," she told them.

Anna thought, maybe being Mimi's pony-sitter wasn't such a good idea after all. Had the Pony Pals taken on a job that they couldn't handle?

Safety First

The next day the Pony Pals rode over to the Off-Main Diner. Anna's mother owned the diner, so the Pony Pals ate there for free. The diner was a perfect place for a Pony Pal meeting.

Pam put in their order for eggs and pancakes. Anna set the table. Lulu poured them all glasses of orange juice. Minutes later, the three girls were sitting in their favorite booth ready to eat and work.

"Mimi doesn't know *anything* about how to take care of a pony," said Anna. "All she wants to do is jump on and ride."

"We have to teach her rules of safety," said Pam.

"And how to groom Tongo," added Anna.

"Let's make a list of what we need to teach her," Lulu suggested.

"Pam, you write the list," said Anna. "You have the best handwriting."

1. Don't stand behind Tongo.

2. Make sure Tongo sees you before you touch him.

3. Brush Tongo.

4. Put on Tongo's tack.

5. Learn to sit in the saddle.

6. Ride with a lead line.

7. Keep gate closed.

"We can do a little of each thing at every lesson," said Pam.

"Starting with safety," said Lulu.

The Pony Pals spent the rest of the morning riding their own ponies.

After lunch, they went over to the Klines' for Mimi's lesson. Mimi was waiting for them on the front porch. She had on riding pants, riding boots, gloves, and a purple helmet.

"Mimi's all excited about her first lesson," said Mrs. Bell. "She was ready two hours ago."

"I'm going to ride my pony," Mimi informed her pony-sitters.

"First, you have to learn some rules of safety," Pam told Mimi.

"No rules," said Mimi.

"You'll like these rules," Anna said. "They're good for you and good for Tongo."

"He's *my* pony," said Mimi.

The Pony Pals exchanged a nervous glance. Teaching Mimi would not be easy.

Mimi and the Pony Pals passed through the gate into the backyard. Tongo was grazing at the other end of the yard.

"A first rule of safety is to always close the gate behind you," Pam told Mimi.

But Mimi didn't hear Pam. She was

running toward Tongo. Anna ran after her. She grabbed Mimi from behind. "Slow down," she said. "There's a rule about how to go up to a pony."

Lulu put a hand on Mimi's shoulder so she wouldn't run off again.

"Never go up to a pony from behind," Pam told Mimi. "Tongo might kick you. He's very strong and it would hurt."

"Tongo won't hurt Mimi," said Mimi. "He's my friend."

Tongo turned and sniffed at Mimi.

Mimi put her arms around Tongo's neck. "I love you," she told him.

"Let's bring Tongo over to the shed," said Pam. "We're going to groom him now."

A few minutes later the Pony Pals were showing Mimi how to brush Tongo. But Mimi wasn't interested. She was feeding Tongo pieces of grass from her open hand.

"Let's give her a ride now," sighed Anna. "She's not paying any attention to the other parts of the lesson."

Anna stayed with Tongo and Mimi while Pam and Lulu went into the shed for the saddle and bridle. Anna brushed Tongo's mane with her fingers. "He's such a good pony," she told Mimi. But Mimi didn't hear her. Anna looked around for the little girl. She found her lying on the ground under Tongo's belly.

"Get up, Mimi," said Anna. "That's a dangerous thing to do."

Mimi didn't move. Anna squatted down. "Tongo might step on you by mistake," she explained.

"Where's his belly button?" asked Mimi.

"Come out and I'll tell you," said Anna.

"I want to *see* it," insisted Mimi.

"Belly buttons on grown ponies don't show," Anna told her.

Pam walked across the paddock with Tongo's saddle. "Mimi, come out now if you want to ride," she said firmly.

Mimi crawled out from under Tongo. Thank goodness Tongo is such a good pony, thought Anna. She held Mimi's

hand while Pam and Lulu saddled up Tongo. When he was ready, Anna gave Mimi a leg up onto the saddle. Pam helped her put her feet in the stirrups. And Lulu showed her how to hold on to the saddle.

"Giddyap," Mimi shouted.

Anna held tight onto Tongo's halter. "I'm going to lead you," Anna told Mimi. "All you have to do is sit still."

"I want to ride by *myself*," she said.

"If you want to ride Tongo you have to do it *our* way," Pam told her.

At first Mimi was unhappy that Anna was leading Tongo. But by the second time up and down the driveway she was having fun. The Pony Pals exchanged smiles. Mimi looked so cute on Tongo!

After they walked the pony and rider up and down the driveway five times, Anna checked her watch. The hour was almost up.

"Is it time to get off?" Mimi asked.

"We call it *dismounting*," explained Pam.

"We have to put fresh water in Tongo's bucket now," Anna said. "And feed him his supper."

"And that will be your lesson for today," added Lulu.

When she was back on the ground, Mimi put her head against Tongo's side. "I want to play with Tongo some more," she said.

"We'll come early tomorrow," Anna told Mimi. "That way you can play with Tongo before your lesson."

A few minutes later, Anna took Mimi inside to Mrs. Bell. She was waiting for Mimi in the kitchen. "I want to play with Tongo," she told Mrs. Bell.

Mrs. Bell shook her head. "You can't, Mimi. I don't know anything about horses."

"Why don't you draw some pictures of Tongo," Anna suggested to Mimi. "You can show them to us tomorrow."

"Okay," said Mimi sadly.

Anna felt sorry for Mimi. She could only be with Tongo when she had a lesson with the Pony Pals. Anna knew that Mimi just wanted to ride Tongo like the Pony Pals rode their ponies. But pony-sitting for Mimi and Tongo was hard work and Anna was very tired.

That night, Anna went out to the paddock to say good night to her own pony. She was giving Acorn a carrot when a brilliant idea flashed into her mind. Acorn could help her with her very difficult pony-sitting job.

My Pony

The next afternoon Anna saddled up Acorn and led him out of the yard and across the Town Green. "You're going to be a pony-sitter today," she told her pony.

Pam and Lulu were already at the Klines'. Lulu, Pam, Mimi, and Tongo were waiting for Anna and Acorn in the middle of the pony enclosure. Acorn and Tongo whinnied hellos to one another.

"Did you tell Mrs. Bell about our plan?" Anna whispered to Lulu.

Lulu smiled and nodded.

"I wanna ride my pony *now*," Mimi said. She stamped her foot.

"You're going to," said Anna. "Lulu is going to lead me and Acorn. And Pam will lead you and Tongo. We'll ride together. You and me."

Anna mounted Acorn. Lulu snapped on the lead rope.

"First, we'll ride around the yard," Anna told Mimi. "Then we have *two* surprises for you."

"Are the surprises for Tongo, too?" asked Mimi.

The Pony Pals laughed. "Yes," said Anna. "They're for Tongo, too. But first we're going to ride on lead."

Pam gave Mimi a leg up. The little girl sat tall and relaxed in the saddle. She kept her feet in the stirrups, heels down.

Acorn was a big help with the pony riding lesson. He did whatever Lulu asked him to do. Walk on. Trot. Or halt. Acorn was showing Tongo what to do. Anna reached over and patted Acorn's neck. "You're a good pony," she said. "I knew I could depend on you."

Acorn nickered softly as if to say, "We're a team."

The two ponies went around the enclosure two times.

"You're doing great, Mimi," Pam said. "Now we can go on the trail behind the library."

"The *trail*!" yelled Mimi.

"You and Mimi lead," Anna called to Pam.

Anna enjoyed being led through the beautiful woods. It was fun to be riding on lead and making Mimi feel good about riding like a Pony Pal.

"Mimi is going to be an excellent rider," Lulu told Anna. "She's a natural."

"And she's having a great time," said Anna.

The trail came out on Belgo Road, right across the street from the Off-Main Diner. It was time for the second surprise for Mimi.

Mimi was sitting up straight in the saddle.

"We're all having a snack at the diner," Anna told Mimi.

"Tongo and Acorn can have a snack too," added Lulu.

The girls crossed the road, tied the two ponies to the hitching post outside the diner, and went inside. Anna carried a plate of brownies to the booth. "This is the official Pony Pal meeting place," Anna told Mimi.

"I'm a Pony Pal," Mimi said proudly.

The Pony Pals exchanged smiles.

After the snack, Anna took Mimi to the kitchen to get some sugar cubes for the ponies. While Pam and Lulu cleared the table, Mimi ran outside to give Acorn and Tongo their treat.

Back at the Klines', the three girls tried to show Mimi how to take off Tongo's tack. But Mimi didn't pay attention. She was more interested in scratching Tongo's nose. When the girls asked Mimi to help brush Tongo, Mimi wanted to chase Tongo around instead. Anna, Pam, and Lulu were getting very frustrated.

Finally, Tongo was brushed and fed, and the Pony Pals brought Mimi inside to Mrs. Bell.

"I want to play with Tongo some more!" Mimi complained to Mrs. Bell.

"Your pony-sitters have to go home for dinner," said Mrs. Bell.

"And to do their homework," added Anna.

"We can't pony-sit tomorrow," Lulu told Mrs. Bell and Mimi. "We have a class field trip to a museum and won't be back until late."

"It won't hurt Mimi to take a day off," said Mrs. Bell.

"I want to play with Tongo," Mimi whined. *"Please!"*

Anna put an arm around Mimi's shoulder. "I'm really sorry, Mimi," Anna said. "We're going to a museum with our class and we won't be back until late."

"After. Pony-sit *after,"* begged Mimi.

"After, we're having dinner at the diner with Lulu's father," said Pam.

"He's going to tell us about his trip to India," Lulu explained. "He was in India studying monkeys."

"I have a monkey!" shouted Mimi. "He's *my* Mr. Monkey." Mimi ran out of the room.

"Mr. Monkey is a stuffed animal," Mrs. Bell explained to the Pony Pals.

In a minute Mimi reappeared with her favorite stuffed animal and a folded piece of drawing paper. Mr. Monkey's fur was almost all worn away, and he had a goofy look on his face. The Pony Pals all shook hands with him anyway.

Mimi handed Anna the drawing paper. "It's a present," she said proudly. Anna unfolded the paper.

"Thank you," said Anna. "It's beautiful. I'll hang it up in my room." When Anna looked up at Mimi she realized that Mimi wasn't listening. She was looking out the kitchen window at Tongo and Acorn. She held up Mr. Monkey so he could see, too. "Wave to Tongo," she told the stuffed animal.

On the bus to the museum the Pony Pals talked about their pony-sitting job.

"We have to teach Mimi so many

things," said Pam. "We've hardly done any of the things on our list."

"It's a harder job than I thought it would be," said Anna.

They talked about Mimi again when they saw a painting with monkeys. There was one monkey that looked just like Mimi's Mr. Monkey!

The Pony Pals were back in Wiggins by six o'clock. It was time to go to the diner with Lulu's father. As they were walking across the Town Green, Anna pointed to the Kline house on Upper Main Street. "Look!" she exclaimed. "There's a police car in front of Mimi's."

A police officer jumped out of the car and ran into the Klines'.

"Why are the police there?" asked Lulu.

"Let's go find out," said Anna.

The Pony Pals ran across the Town Green to Upper Main Street. As she ran, Anna felt her heart beating. She was terribly afraid — afraid that something awful had happened to Mimi.

Missing!

The front door to the Klines' house was wide-open. The girls followed the sound of voices to the kitchen. Anna saw Mrs. Bell sitting in a chair. She'd been crying. Next, she saw Mr. and Mrs. Kline and the police officer standing near the sink. They were talking.

"What happened?" Anna blurted out.

Mrs. Kline swung around to the Pony Pals. "Is Mimi with you?" she asked.

"No," said Pam. "We just got back from our school trip."

Mrs. Kline sank into a chair. She started to cry. Mr. Kline put his hand on her shoulder. "Don't worry," he said. "We'll find her."

Mrs. Bell looked up. "Mimi was playing in the living room," she told the Pony Pals. "I went to the kitchen to empty the dishwasher. When I came back, she was gone. I looked everywhere. Then I called her parents . . . and the police."

"Have you checked the neighbors' houses?" the police officer said.

"We just got here a minute ahead of you, Officer Hunter," Mrs. Kline answered. "Our daughter is only five years old."

"The door wasn't locked," Mr. Kline said. "Someone could have walked in and . . ."

Anna was thinking the same thing. What if someone had kidnapped Mimi?

"Maybe she wandered off by herself," said Pam.

"Or went to visit a friend," suggested Anna.

"Mrs. Kline, why don't you and Mrs. Bell ask the neighbors if they've seen your little girl," said Officer Hunter.

"Good idea," said Mrs. Kline. "It's a place to start." Mrs. Kline and Mrs. Bell went to check the neighborhood.

Mr. Kline pointed to the Pony Pals. "Officer, these girls have been taking care of Mimi and her pony in the afternoons," he said.

"Do you girls have any idea where Mimi might have gone?" Officer Hunter asked.

Anna looked out at the backyard. "Well, her pony's gone, too," she said.

"Mimi must have taken him with her — wherever she went," said Lulu.

"So she wasn't kidnapped," said Pam. "Kidnappers wouldn't take her pony, too."

Mr. Kline paced the kitchen. "It's already after six o'clock," he said. "We have to find her before night falls. What if she's trying to ride? That pony could hurt her."

"Mimi's too little to put on a saddle and

bridle by herself," said Pam. "So if she's riding, it's bareback."

And bareback riding is even more dangerous, thought Anna.

"Do you girls have any idea where she might go with a pony?" Officer Hunter asked.

"Mimi knew that we were on a school trip," said Lulu. "Maybe she went to school to look for us."

"Or she might have gone on the trail we took yesterday," said Anna. "It starts behind the library and goes to Belgo Road."

"And we have our own trail that starts behind Anna's house," said Lulu. "That's 26 Main Street. The trail goes all the way to Crandal's Animal Hospital on Riddle Road."

"I told Mimi I'd take her riding there someday," added Anna.

Mrs. Bell and Mrs. Kline came in through the kitchen door. Anna knew by the looks on their faces that they hadn't found Mimi. "Mrs. Bell checked with the

Thompsons and I went over to the Shapiros'," said Mrs. Kline. "They haven't seen her. They're going house-to-house to ask our other neighbors."

"It's time to organize a search party for the woods," said Officer Hunter. "We'll check out those trails, too."

"We'll help," said Anna.

"You've helped us plenty already," said the officer. "Go home now. We don't need to have *four* lost children."

The Pony Pals exchanged a glance. They silently agreed not to argue with Officer Hunter.

"We'll let you know when we find her," Mrs. Kline told the Pony Pals. "Thank you."

The Pony Pals left the Klines and had an emergency Pony Pal meeting on the sidewalk.

"That police officer thinks we'd get lost looking for Mimi," said Lulu. "I hate that."

"Let's start our search behind the library," said Pam.

"And look for evidence on the trail," added Lulu.

"It'll be dark soon," said Anna. "We'd better hurry."

The girls ran around the library to the parking lot. "Let's see if there's any pony plop here," said Anna. "That would be a big clue."

There wasn't any pony plop. But they went on the trail anyway.

"You two run ahead," suggested Lulu. "I'll walk and look for small clues. She might have gone off the trail." Lulu reached in her pocket and took out her whistle. "I'll blow one long whistle if I find anything."

"Good," said Pam.

Anna took her whistle out of her backpack and hung it around her neck. "And if one of them is injured, we'll use the S.O.S. signal," she said.

"If you whistle, I'll go back and tell everyone that we found them," said Lulu.

Anna and Pam ran single file along the

trail. "Mimi," they called out. "Where are you, Mimi?"

As she was running, Anna thought, it's *my* fault that Mimi is lost. I'm the one who was supposed to teach her about safety. I'm the one who let her think she could be a Pony Pal. It's all my fault.

Anna looked left and right as she ran. Where are you, Mimi? she wondered. Are you hurt?

Mr. Monkey

Anna and Pam ran along the trail.

"Mimi!" Anna shouted at the top of her lungs.

Suddenly, Anna stopped in her tracks. She saw someone at the edge of the trail. Pam saw her, too. It was Mimi! She was squatting behind a bush and holding tight to Mr. Monkey.

"Mimi!" Anna exclaimed. "We've been looking for you."

"Sh-hh," Mimi told Anna.

"Are you all right?" asked Pam.

"Sh-shh," Mimi repeated. "I'm hiding."

Who was Mimi hiding from? Anna wondered. Was some mean person chasing her? She remembered how Tommy Rand liked to trick and tease younger kids. Maybe Mimi was hiding from Tommy Rand. Or maybe she was afraid of an animal in the woods.

Anna and Pam squatted next to Mimi. Anna put her arm around Mimi's shoulders.

"Don't worry," Pam said. "We're here now. We'll take care of you."

"Where's Tongo?" Anna asked Mimi.

"I dunno," answered Mimi. "It's my turn to hide."

Anna and Pam exchanged a smile.

"Are you playing hide-and-seek with Tongo?" Anna asked.

"You can play, too," Mimi whispered.

Anna heard a nicker. Through the bushes she saw Tongo coming toward them on the trail. He sniffed the air and trotted closer. Then he stuck his nose in the bush.

Mimi jumped up and yelled, "Surprise!" and shook Mr. Monkey in Tongo's face.

Tongo took a step back, but he wasn't spooked. He was used to playing with children.

Pam took hold of Tongo's halter. "Good pony," she told him.

Anna blew one long whistle so Lulu would know that they'd found Mimi.

Pam took Mimi's hand. "You shouldn't have run away," she said.

"Your mother and father and Mrs. Bell are very worried about you," added Anna.

"Where's the lead rope, Mimi?" asked Pam.

"No rope," said Mimi.

"Tongo must have just followed her," Anna told Pam.

"Tongo follows me everywhere," said Mimi proudly.

"Then he'll follow you home," said Pam.

"I don't want to go home!" cried Mimi.

"We're going to the diner. Lulu's dad took pictures of monkeys." She held up her stuffed animal. "Mr. Monkey wants to see the pictures."

"Mimi," said Pam in a firm voice. "You have to go home *now*."

"No!" shouted Mimi.

"It's time for Tongo's oats," said Anna. "He wants *his* dinner."

Mimi looked from Anna to Tongo. She wrinkled up her forehead and thought for a second. "I can't play with you anymore," she told Anna and Pam. "I have to go home. Tongo's hungry."

"I'll give you a ride," said Pam. She turned her back to Mimi and bent over. "Hop on."

Mimi put her arms around Pam's neck and her legs around Pam's waist. She was careful not to wrap them too tight. Mimi handed Mr. Monkey to Anna. "Mr. Monkey can ride on Tongo," she said.

Anna stuck Mr. Monkey's legs in the halter between Tongo's ears so the mon-

48

key was sitting up straight. They started back on the trail to Mimi's house.

A minute later they heard running feet. Happy voices yelled, "Mimi!"

Soon Mr. and Mrs. Kline and Lulu were gathered round them. Mimi's parents hugged and kissed her. And they thanked the Pony Pals over and over again for finding their little girl.

Mimi rode on her father's shoulders the rest of the way home. Tongo tagged along behind them.

Officer Hunter was waiting for them on the Klines' porch. "I've called off all the search parties," she said. "I guess we can say this case is closed."

"Thanks to the Pony Pals," said Mrs. Kline.

Officer Hunter turned to the Pony Pals. "So you three didn't go home after all," she said.

"Not yet," said Anna.

Lulu looked at her watch. "My father's going to wonder where we are," she said.

"I'd better go home or he'll send out a search party for *us*."

"We'll meet you at the diner," Anna whispered to Lulu.

Pam, Anna, and Mimi took Tongo around to his paddock. Mimi helped put out his water and oats. Then Mimi gave her pony a final hug and said good night to him.

When they were back in the house, Mrs. Kline took Mimi upstairs for a bath. Anna and Pam stood at the front door with Mr. Kline. "What a scare we had," he said. "I was imagining all sorts of horrible things."

"Me, too," said Anna.

"Mimi was acting like a Pony Pal," said Pam. "But she's too young and inexperienced to go on trails alone."

"That's for sure," said Mr. Kline. He handed Anna an envelope. "Here's our payment to the Pony Pals for pony-sitting."

"Thank you," said Anna. "I have tutoring tomorrow. But Lulu and Pam can come right after school."

"We'll concentrate on safety in our lessons," said Pam.

"We won't be needing pony-sitters anymore," Mr. Kline said. "We're giving the pony back to Mr. Olson first thing in the morning."

"I'm sure Mimi won't run away again," said Pam.

"And she loves Tongo so much," added Anna.

"We can't take a chance," said Mr. Kline. "We think that Mimi is too young to have a pony."

Anna and Pam said good night to Mr. Kline. Then they walked over to the diner to meet Lulu and her father.

Mr. Sanders' photos of monkeys were terrific. And it was interesting to learn about them. But during the dinner, Anna's mind kept going back to Mimi and Tongo. It's my fault, she thought. Mimi and Tongo are going to be separated because of me.

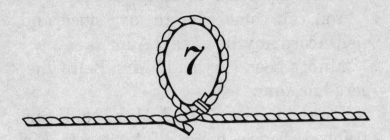

Where's My Pony?

Anna thought a lot about Mimi over the next couple of days. She knew that Mimi must be very upset about losing her pony.

Friday, on the way home from school, the Pony Pals met Mrs. Bell and Mimi walking across the Town Green.

"I'm so happy to see you girls," Mrs. Bell said. "We miss your afternoon visits."

"Where's Tongo?" Mimi asked sadly. "I miss my pony. I want to see him."

"Tongo went back to Mr. Olson's," Mrs. Bell said. "You know that."

"I miss my pony," Mimi repeated.

"You can come over to my house and visit Acorn anytime," said Anna.

"Mimi's been *very* sad," Mrs. Bell whispered to Anna.

"I want to see Tongo!" Mimi said. She grabbed Anna's hand. "Take me to Mr. Olson's. *Please!*" she pleaded.

"We can't take you to Mr. Olson's without your parents' permission," said Anna.

"Tell them," said Mimi. "Tell them I can go."

The Pony Pals exchanged a glance.

"I suppose we could walk over to the hardware store and ask," said Lulu.

"Is that okay with you?" Pam asked Mrs. Bell.

"Certainly," she answered. "We'll go back to the house and wait for you."

Mrs. Kline wasn't at the hardware store. But Mr. Kline was there. He invited the Pony Pals into his office. There were only two chairs, so the girls stood. Mr. Kline sat on the edge of his desk.

"So what can I do for the Pony Pals?" he asked.

"We met Mimi and Mrs. Bell on the Town Green," began Lulu.

"And Mimi told us she wanted to visit Tongo," said Pam.

"We'll take her there, if it's okay with you," added Anna.

"She misses Tongo so much," said Lulu.

"I feel awful about taking Mimi's pony away," he said sadly. "But she can't visit him. She has to forget about that pony. Please, don't put ideas in her head."

"It was Mimi's idea to visit him," Pam said.

"I'm sure it was," he said. "But I think it would help if you girls don't talk about ponies around her."

"We won't," Lulu promised.

"We'll try to get her to think about something else," added Pam.

"She likes to draw," said Anna. "I'll draw with her."

"That would be great," Mr. Kline said.

"I'm sure Mimi would like that."

The Pony Pals left the hardware store and went over to Mimi's house. She was waiting for the Pony Pals on the porch with Mrs. Bell.

Mimi ran down the porch steps to meet them. She had on her riding clothes and was carrying her purple helmet in one hand and Mr. Monkey in the other. "I'm going to play with Tongo," she said.

"Your dad said you can't go over to Mr. Olson's," said Pam.

Mimi twisted up her face. Anna knew that she had to act fast before Mimi started to cry.

"I have an idea!" Anna exclaimed. "Let's draw some pictures."

"I don't want to draw," whined Mimi. "I want Tongo!"

Anna squatted in front of Mimi. "I have some neat colored pencils," she said. "You can use them."

"Okay," said Mimi.

Mimi went to the kitchen with Mrs. Bell

and the Pony Pals. But she was still sad.

Anna and Mimi sat at the kitchen table to draw. Pam and Lulu poured juice and Mrs. Bell put a plate of cookies on the table.

Anna looked over to see how Mimi's drawing was coming along, but Mimi blocked her drawing with her arms. "Don't look," she scolded.

After eating some cookies, the Pony Pals said goodbye to Mrs. Bell and Mimi. "I'll come draw with you again sometime," Anna told Mimi.

Mimi handed Anna her folded-up drawing. "It's for you," she whispered.

The Pony Pals left the Klines'. They walked to a sunny spot on the Town Green and sat on the grass. Anna opened up Mimi's drawing and they looked at it together.

"That's so sad," said Lulu.

"She lost her pony because of me," Anna said.

"That's not true," said Lulu.

"It wasn't your fault," added Pam.

"I didn't teach her enough about safety," said Anna. "I let her think she could be a Pony Pal."

"We were *all* pony-sitters," said Lulu. "We were all responsible for Mimi and Tongo."

"She really loved that little pony," said Anna.

"Remember when your parents said you couldn't keep Acorn?" Pam asked Anna.

"We got Acorn back for you," said Lulu. "Now we have to get Tongo back for Mimi."

"How can we convince Mimi's parents to take Tongo back?" asked Anna.

"It's time for three ideas," said Lulu.

Pam checked her watch. "I have to go home," she said. "I promised my mother I'd work with her school ponies."

"Let's all work on our ideas tonight," said Lulu. "And we'll meet first thing tomorrow morning."

Anna didn't have any ideas about how they could get Tongo back for Mimi. Was this a problem that the Pony Pals couldn't solve?

Three Ideas

Early the next morning, Anna and Lulu saddled up their ponies and rode onto Pony Pal trail. They met Pam at the three birch trees. It was time for a Pony Pal meeting to solve the problem of Mimi and Tongo.

"Let's have our meeting near the waterfall," suggested Lulu.

The Pony Pals turned onto the Wiggins Estate Trail. Anna loved riding on the trails and through the open field. She saw squirrels, rabbits, and even some wild turkeys. Snow White and Lightning were spooked when the flock of turkeys flew up around them. But, as usual, nothing spooked Acorn. Anna thought, Tongo is a lot like Acorn. I bet he wouldn't spook either. Tongo's the perfect pony for a little girl like Mimi.

Soon the ponies were drinking from Badd Brook, and the Pony Pals were sitting on rocks watching the waterfall.

"Lulu, you go first," said Anna.

Lulu took a piece of paper out of her jacket pocket and handed it to Pam. Pam read Lulu's idea out loud.

Tell the Klines that Mimi wasn't lost.

"You're right," said Pam. "The Klines probably think that Mimi was lost."

"We should tell them that she knew her way home," said Lulu. "So it wasn't so dangerous for her to be on the trail."

"I think she would have come home

when it started to get dark," added Anna. "We should tell them that, too."

"What's your idea, Anna?" asked Lulu.

Anna opened up a piece of drawing paper and showed it to Lulu and Pam.

"Tongo was Mimi's pet," said Anna. "She wanted to hang out with him."

"The only time she could be with Tongo was when we were there," said Pam. "But she wanted to play with him a lot more than that."

"That's *really* why she left home," said Lulu. "So she could play with her pony."

"If she could play with Tongo at home," said Pam, "then she'd stay in her own backyard with Mrs. Bell or her parents."

"But Mrs. Bell doesn't know how to take care of Mimi when she's with a pony," said Lulu.

"We could teach her," said Pam. "My mom would help, too."

"Mrs. Bell wouldn't have to give riding lessons," said Anna. "That would still be our job."

"Do you think Mrs. Bell would agree?" asked Lulu.

"I think so," said Anna. "She's sad that Mimi is so unhappy. She wants to help her."

"What's your idea, Pam?" asked Anna.

Pam handed her idea to Anna. Anna read it out loud.

Ask Mr. Olson not to sell Tongo to someone else.

"What if Mimi's parents decided to buy back Tongo and he was gone?" said Anna. "That would be the worst!"

"Maybe he's sold Tongo already!" exclaimed Lulu.

"We'd better find out," said Pam.

"Pam, why don't you go see Mr. Olson," said Anna. "And Lulu and I will go tell our ideas to the Klines."

Pam stood up. "Let's go," she said.

The three girls rode to Snow White and Acorn's paddock. Lulu and Anna put their ponies in the field. But Pam stayed on Lightning.

"Tell Mr. Olson what a good rider Mimi is going to be," Lulu told Pam.

"And that she already loves him very much," added Anna.

"And say hi to Tongo for us," said Lulu.

"I will," said Pam. "If Tongo is still there."

After Pam and Lightning left, Anna

gave her own pony a hug. It was time to talk to the Klines.

"Wish us luck, Acorn," Anna said.

Acorn nuzzled Anna's shoulder.

"Thanks," said Anna.

But Anna still felt nervous. She and Lulu had to convince Mimi's parents to buy back Tongo. If they didn't, Mimi and Tongo would be separated forever.

Giddyap!

Anna and Lulu walked onto Main Street. "Should we go to the Klines' house or the hardware store?" Lulu asked.

Anna looked across the Town Green. "Their pickup truck is parked in the driveway," she said. "Let's go see who's home."

The two girls ran across the green and up the porch steps.

Lulu rang the doorbell. Mrs. Kline came to the door.

"Hi, girls," she said. "How are you?"

"Fine," answered Lulu.

"Come on in," said Mrs. Kline. "Mimi is out back playing with Rosalie Lacey."

Rosalie was a six-year-old who was a good friend of the Pony Pals. Rosalie loved ponies as much as Mimi.

"How is Mimi?" Anna asked Mrs. Kline.

"Not very good," answered Mrs. Kline. "She's still unhappy that we took her pony away."

"That's what we came to talk to you about," said Lulu.

Anna and Lulu followed Mrs. Kline into the kitchen. Mr. Kline was sitting at the table. He invited the girls to sit down.

"Anna and Lulu want to talk to us about Mimi," said Mrs. Kline.

As she sat down, Anna heard someone yelling, "Giddyap!" Through the kitchen window she saw Mimi and Rosalie. They were playing in the backyard. Rosalie was on her hands and knees. She was the pony. Mimi sat on Rosalie's back. She was the rider. It reminded Anna of when she used to play with her older sister.

"We invited Rosalie over to help Mimi forget about ponies," said Mr. Kline. "I guess it's not working."

"I didn't realize how upset Mimi would be when we gave Tongo back," said Mrs. Kline.

"We had no choice," Mr. Kline told his wife. "It was too dangerous, especially when she ran away with Tongo and got lost."

"Actually, we don't think Mimi was lost," said Lulu.

"We took Mimi and Tongo on that trail the day before," said Anna. "I'm sure they both knew the way home."

"And Mimi didn't really run away, either," said Lulu. "She just wanted to be with her pony."

"She couldn't be with Tongo unless we were pony-sitting," said Anna.

"If you and Mrs. Bell could learn how to pony-sit," said Anna. "Then Mimi could be with Tongo a lot more."

"It's not hard to learn," said Lulu.

"Pam's mother is a riding teacher. She could help show you what to do so Mimi will always be safe."

Mrs. Kline looked out the window. Mimi was now pretending Rosalie was a cart pony. She was using Tongo's lead rope for the driving reins.

"Mrs. Bell is worried about Mimi and wants her happy again," said Mrs. Kline. "She might be willing to learn how to pony-sit."

"I'm still worried about Mimi being with such a big animal," Mr. Kline said.

"Mimi will keep growing," Anna pointed out. "Tongo will always be a small pony."

"We'll think about what you've said," Mrs. Kline told the Pony Pals.

"But we need to talk privately about this," added Mr. Kline.

"We'll go out back and see Rosalie and Mimi," said Lulu.

"But, please, don't talk too much about ponies," said Mrs. Kline.

"Okay," agreed Anna.

Lulu and Anna walked out to the backyard. Mimi drove Rosalie-the-pony over to them. Rosalie whinnied. Anna patted her head. "Nice pony," she said laughing.

"Can we go see Acorn?" asked Rosalie. "I want to ride him."

"Not today," Anna told Rosalie.

"I want Tongo!" said Mimi. Tears came into her eyes. "I want my pony. He misses me."

"I know," said Anna.

"We'll play a game with you," said Lulu. "What do you want to play?"

"How about hide-and-seek?" asked Rosalie.

"I want to play with Tongo!" repeated Mimi.

Just then a pony came into the yard. But it wasn't Tongo. Pam was leading Lightning toward them. She raised her hand in an okay sign. Anna knew it meant Tongo was still at Mr. Olson's. Now if only Mr. and Mrs. Kline would say they would buy him back for Mimi!

On Library Trail

Pam and Lightning walked over to Lulu, Anna, Rosalie, and Mimi. Rosalie ran up to Lightning and rubbed her upside-down heart. Mr. and Mrs. Kline came out to the yard, too.

"Well, Mimi," Mr. Kline said. "You have lots of company here today."

"But I want Tongo, Daddy," Mimi said sadly.

"Mimi," said Mr. Kline, "do you know why you don't have Tongo anymore?"

Mimi thought for a second. "Because

74

Mr. Monkey and Tongo ran away," she said.

"No," her mother said, "because *you* ran away."

"I didn't, Mommy," said Mimi. "I didn't run away. Mr. Monkey wanted to see the monkeys."

"Mimi, there are no real monkeys in the woods around here," said Mr. Kline.

"Mimi *is* talking about *real* monkeys," said Anna. "She knew that we were having dinner with Lulu's father at the Off-Main Diner. And he was going to show us pictures that he took of monkeys."

"My dad studied them in India," said Lulu. "Mimi — and Mr. Monkey — wanted to see the pictures."

Mr. and Mrs. Kline exchanged glances. They nodded at one another.

Mrs. Kline squatted in front of Mimi and held her hands. "Mimi," she said. "Do you promise never, ever, to run away again?"

Mimi nodded. "I promise," she said.

Mimi put her arms around her mother's neck. "Mommy," she said. "I want Tongo. Can he come back? *Please.*"

"Yes," said Mrs. Kline. "He can."

"If Mr. Olson still has him," added Mr. Kline.

"He does!" shouted the Pony Pals in unison.

"I went over to Olson's farm," Pam explained. She smiled. "I told Mr. Olson you might want Tongo back."

"The Pony Pals think of everything," said Mr. Kline.

"Well, let's go get him," said Mrs. Kline. "I've missed that cute little pony, too."

"Yea!" shouted Mimi.

"Now, hold on, everyone," Mr. Kline said. He shook a finger at Mimi. "There are rules to be kept, young lady," he said sternly. "And you have to follow them."

Mimi shook a finger at Mr. Monkey. "There are rules to be kept, young monkey," she said. "And you have to follow them."

Pam covered her mouth so Mimi wouldn't see her laugh.

Lulu turned a laugh into a cough.

And Anna covered her face with her arm.

Mrs. Kline doubled over with laughter, and pretended to tie her shoe.

Mr. Kline managed to keep a straight face. "You *and* Mr. Monkey must both keep the rules," he said.

"I know, Daddy," said Mimi. She lowered her voice to a whisper. "And I know Mr. Monkey isn't real. But don't tell him."

"Okay," Mr. Kline whispered back.

"I'll go in and call Mr. Olson," said Mrs. Kline, "and tell him we want to buy Tongo back."

"We can go get Tongo for you," said Anna. "We'll pony him back like the last time."

Mr. Kline looked at his watch. "We have to go back to work soon," he said. "But Mrs. Bell will be here any minute." He smiled at the Pony Pals. "We already spoke to her about pony-sitting. She agreed to learn."

"That's terrific," said Lulu.

"We can pony-sit this afternoon," said Pam. "That way we can begin Mrs. Bell's lessons."

"Can I help?" asked Rosalie.

"Yes," said Anna. "And Acorn will help, too."

The Pony Pals rode their ponies on the trail behind the library. Soon, they were riding back on that same trail with Tongo. They were halfway to the Klines' when Mimi came running along the trail toward them.

"Tongo! Tongo!" she yelled.

The Pony Pals halted their ponies and dismounted.

"Mimi," Anna said. "You aren't supposed to be here. They'll make you give Tongo back again."

"Everyone is going to be worried about you," said Lulu.

"And angry," added Pam.

Just then, Mrs. Bell and Rosalie came around the turn in the trail.

"That girl!" exclaimed Mrs. Bell. "We were all coming to meet you. Mimi ran ahead of me the whole way. She has more energy than a million batteries." She lowered her voice. "I'm so glad Mimi's got her pony back," she whispered to Anna.

"Me, too," said Anna.

Mimi ran up to Tongo and gave him a big hug. "*My* pony!" she said. "You're *my* pony."

Tongo gave a nicker as if to say, "And you're my Pony Pal."

Dear Reader,

I am having a lot of fun researching and writing books about the Pony Pals. I've met many interesting kids and adults who love ponies. And I've visited some wonderful ponies at homes, farms, and riding schools.

Before writing Pony Pals I wrote fourteen novels for children and young adults. Four of these were honored by Children's Choice Awards.

I live in Sharon, Connecticut, with my husband, Lee, and our dog, Willie. Our daughter is all grown up and has her own apartment in New York City.

Besides writing novels I like to draw, paint, garden and swim. I didn't have a pony when I was growing up, but I have always loved them and dreamt about riding. Now I take riding lessons on a horse named Saz. To learn more, visit my Web site: www.jeannebetancourt.com.

I like reading and writing about ponies as much as I do riding. Which proves to me that you don't have to ride a pony to love them. And you certainly don't need a pony to be a Pony Pal.

Happy Reading,

Jeanne Betancourt

PONY PALS

Be a Pony Pal!®

❏ BBC0-590-48583-0	#1	I Want a Pony	$2.99
❏ BBC0-590-48584-9	#2	A Pony for Keeps	$2.99
❏ BBC0-590-48585-7	#3	A Pony in Trouble	$2.99
❏ BBC0-590-48586-5	#4	Give Me Back My Pony	$2.99
❏ BBC0-590-25244-5	#5	Pony to the Rescue	$2.99
❏ BBC0-590-25245-3	#6	Too Many Ponies	$2.99
❏ BBC0-590-54338-5	#7	Runaway Pony	$2.99
❏ BBC0-590-54339-3	#8	Good-bye Pony	$2.99
❏ BBC0-590-62974-3	#9	The Wild Pony	$2.99
❏ BBC0-590-62975-1	#10	Don't Hurt My Pony	$2.99
❏ BBC0-590-86597-8	#11	Circus Pony	$2.99
❏ BBC0-590-86598-6	#12	Keep Out, Pony!	$2.99
❏ BBC0-590-86600-1	#13	The Girl Who Hated Ponies	$2.99
❏ BBC0-590-86601-X	#14	Pony-Sitters	$3.50
❏ BBC0-590-86632-X	#15	The Blind Pony	$3.50
❏ BBC0-590-37459-1	#16	The Missing Pony Pal	$3.50
❏ BBC0-590-37460-5	#17	Detective Pony	$3.50
❏ BBC0-590-51295-1	#18	The Saddest Pony	$3.50
❏ BBC0-590-63397-X	#19	Moving Pony	$3.50
❏ BBC0-590-63401-1	#20	Stolen Ponies	$3.50
❏ BBC0-590-63405-4	#21	The Winning Pony	$3.50
❏ BBC0-590-74210-8		Pony Pals Super Special #1: The Baby Pony	$5.99
❏ BBC0-590-86631-1		Pony Pals Super Special #2: The Lives of our Ponies	$5.99
❏ BBC0-590-37461-3		Pony Pals Super Special #3: The Ghost Pony	$5.99

Available wherever you buy books, or use this order form.

....

Send orders to Scholastic Inc., P.O. Box 7500, Jefferson City, MO 65102

Please send me the books I have checked above. I am enclosing $_____ (please add $2.00 to cover shipping and handling). Send check or money order — no cash or C.O.D.s please.

Please allow four to six weeks for delivery. Offer good in the U.S.A. only. Sorry, mail orders are not available to residents of Canada. Prices subject to change.

Name_____ Birthdate ___/___/___

First   Last   M   D   Y

Address_____

City_____ State_____ Zip_____

Telephone (   ) _____ ❏ Boy   ❏ Girl

Where did you buy this book?   ❏ Bookstore   ❏ Book Fair   ❏ Book Club   ❏ Other   PP399